Detective Danny and the Mystery of the Missing Necklace

by *Abderrahim Nouh*

COPYRIGHT © 2024

AUTHOR: ABDERRAHIM NOUH

ALL RIGHTS RESERVED.NO PART OF THIS BOOK MAY BE REPRODUCED,DISTRIBUTED, OR TRANSMITTED IN ANY FORM OR BY ANY MEANS, INCLUDING PHOTOCOPYING, RECORDING OR OTHER ELECTRONIC OR MECHANICAL METHODS,WITHOUT THE PRIOR WRITTEN PERMISSION FROM THE AUTHOR, EXCEPT IN THE CASE OF BRIEF QUOTATIONS EMBODIED IN CRITICAL REVIEWS AND CERTAIN OTHER NONCOMMERCIAL USES PERMITTED BY COPYRIGHT LAW.

THIS BOOK IS A WORK OF FICTION. NAMES, CHARACTERS, BUSINESSES, ORGANIZATIONS, PLACES, EVENTS AND INCIDENTS ARE EITHER THE PRODUCT OF THE AUTHOR'S IMAGINATION OR USED FICTITIOUSLY.ANY RESEMBLANCE TO ACTUAL PERSONS, LIVING OR DEAD, EVENTS OR LOCALS IS ENTIRELY COINCIDENTAL.

Table of Contents

Introduction

In the picturesque town of Midrock, where mysteries are hidden in every nook and cranny, lives Danny, a 10-year-old boy with an extraordinary dream. Danny aspires to become a detective, and his heart is brimming with curiosity and an insatiable hunger for adventure. His sharp mind and keen eyes have earned him a reputation as the area's unofficial detective. He has tackled mysteries and solved secrets that have left others baffled, becoming a local hero in the process.

One sunny morning, the peaceful atmosphere of Midrock is shattered when Mr. Walker's priceless necklace, The Rose of Midrock, disappears from his jewelry shop. The necklace, known for its breathtaking beauty and historical significance, had been the pride of Midrock. Its sudden disappearance sends shockwaves through the town, leaving everyone in a state of confusion and concern.

The Rose of Midrock is more than just a piece of jewelry; it is a symbol of the town's heritage and elegance. Crafted with exquisite detail and adorned with precious gems, the necklace had captivated the hearts of Midrock's residents for generations. Now, it has become the focal point of a mysterious case that has everyone puzzled and anxious for answers.

Determined to solve the case, Danny teams up with his best friend and loyal assistant, Katy. At 9 years old, Katy shares Danny's enthusiasm for solving mysteries. With her quick thinking and keen observations, she is the perfect partner for Danny. Together, they make an unstoppable team, ready to take on the challenge of finding the missing necklace.

As Danny and Katy embark on their most difficult mission yet, their bond grows stronger. Each step they take deepens their friendship and sharpens their resolve. Working together teaches them valuable lessons about companionship, perseverance, and the importance of believing in oneself. The mystery of The Rose of Midrock becomes a journey of self-discovery and growth for both young detectives.

"Detective Danny and The Mystery of the Missing Necklace" is a charming and exciting story set in a town filled with charm and secrets. Join Danny and Katy as they unravel the truth behind the baffling case, uncover the hidden history of the necklace, and venture into a world where every twist and turn leads to a heartwarming conclusion. Get ready for a captivating journey of mystery, friendship, and the joy of seeking truth in the delightful town of Midrock.

Chapter 1: The Call for Help

One brilliant morning, as the sun shone upon the dew-kissed grass, Danny was playing with his friends in the town's enchanting little park. The fresh morning light made everything look magical. The grass sparkled with tiny droplets of dew, adding to the beauty of the park.

The air was filled with the sounds of children chuckling and laughing. Their joy and energy made the whole park feel even more wonderful. The children's happiness was contagious, and it seemed like nothing could spoil the cheerful atmosphere.

However,beneath the surface of this joyful scene, a feeling of stress was quietly lurking. Despite the fun and laughter, there was an underlying tension that couldn't be ignored. It was like a shadow that hid behind the bright morning, unnoticed by these children.

Mr. Walker, the town's beloved jewelry maker, walked toward the children with a grieved look on his face. He was well-loved in the community and known for his cheerful personality. Usually, he always had a smile that made everyone feel happy.

Today,however, something was different. Mr. Walker's usual smile was gone. Instead, there was a look of concern on his face. It was clear that something was troubling him deeply.

As he approached the children, his worried expression stood out. The change in his demeanor was noticeable, making everyone wonder what had happened to cause such sadness in someone usually so joyful.

Danny's curiosity was piqued, and he walked toward Mr. Walker with a serious look on his face. "What's wrong, Mr. Walker?" he asked, his voice full of concern. He could tell that something was seriously troubling the kind jewelry maker.

"Oh, Danny," Mr. Walker murmured, "Last night, while I was away , something terrible happened.Someone broke into jewelry shop and stole the most precious necklace found in the shop." His voice was filled with sadness and worry as he shared the bad news with Danny and the other children.

The kids were out of breath, knowing how important Mr. Walker's work was. They knew that his craftsmanship was amazing and that his jewelry was worn by nobles and famous people all over the country. His pieces were highly valued and admired by many.

Mr. Walker then spoke about a particular necklace. He explained that it was not just priceless but also meant to be the centerpiece of the upcoming jewelry exhibition. The necklace was very special and important for the event, making its loss a big problem.

Mr. Walker looked worried as he continued to speak."I've looked all over, yet I can't find it anywhere," he said. Turning to Danny, he asked, "Please, Danny, can you help me find it? I don't know what to do if it is lost forever." The kids could see the worry in his eyes and understood how much finding the necklace meant to him.

Without hesitation, Danny nodded solemnly."Of course, Mr. Walker. You can count on me. I'll find your necklace and bring it back to you, " he promised.

Mr. Walker's eyes sparkled with gratitude as he clasped his hands together. "Thank you, Danny," he said with a heartfelt tone. "I always knew I could count on you." His voice was filled with warmth and hope, reflecting how much he trusted Danny to help him.

"Please, give it your best effort," Mr. Walker continued. "If you need any help during your investigation, don't hesitate to ask." He wanted Danny to know that he was there to support him in any way he could, and he appreciated the young detective's willingness to step up.

With a fresh sense of purpose,Danny said goodbye to his friends and headed towards Mr. Walker's jewelry shop. He felt the weight of the task ahead on his young shoulders, knowing it was a big responsibility. Despite the pressure, he was determined to do his best.

Danny understood that finding the stolen necklace was important for more reasons than just its value. He knew it had a special meaning to Mr. Walker, and that made the task even more significant. He was committed to solving the case and finding the necklace for Mr. Walker, who had always been kind and trusted him.

As Danny stepped into the jewelry shop , he was greeted by the strong scent of polished silver and sparkling gems. The smell filled the air, reminding him of the shop's precious treasures. He carefully began to examine the area, determined to find any clues that might help him locate the missing necklace.

Danny's sharp eyes scanned every corner of the room. He looked closely at everything, from the faint footprints on the floor to the slightly open window. He paid attention to every small detail, knowing that even the tiniest piece of information could be important in solving the mystery. His focus was intense as he searched for any sign that could lead him to the missing jewelry.

Thus began Detective Danny's adventure as he set out on the quest to find the stolen necklace. He knew that this case would lead him on an exciting journey, one that would challenge his skills and flexibility more than any case before. The task ahead was daunting, but Danny was ready for the challenge.

Danny was aware that this investigation would not be easy. He would need to use all his abilities and stay sharp throughout the process. Despite the difficulties, he remained determined to solve the mystery. He was confident that his hard work and attention to detail would help him succeed.

The young detective was motivated by his goal of bringing the missing necklace back to Mr. Walker. Danny hoped to restore happiness not only to Mr. Walker but also to the entire town of Midrock. With a strong sense of purpose, he was ready to tackle the challenge and make a difference.

Chapter 2: The Clues Unraveled

The sun was high in the sky,bathing Midrock in warm,golden light as Detective Danny continued his investigation into the missing necklace. With determination in his heart and his trusty magnifying glass in hand, he returned to the jewelry shop to take another look.

Danny carefully re-examined every part of the shop, paying close attention to every corner. His keen eyes swept across the floor, the walls, and even the display cases, looking for any small detail that he might have missed earlier. He was thorough in his search, knowing that finding the slightest clue could be crucial to solving the case.

As Danny got closer to the display where the necklace used to be, he noticed a faint but noticeable fragrance in the air. The smell was delicate, and it caught his attention immediately. He took a moment to focus on the scent, trying to identify it.

Danny closed his eyes and took a deep breath, realizing that the aroma was lavender. He had encountered this sweet smell before and recognized it right away. As he thought about the lavender scent, his mind began to race, wondering why it was present in the jewelry shop.

"Why is there lavender here?" Danny whispered to himself. The presence of lavender seemed unusual and out of place, making him curious. He knew that this scent might be an important clue, so he decided to investigate further to understand its significance in the case.

Danny's thoughts wandered to people he knew who loved the scent of lavender. He remembered that several of his friends and acquaintances enjoyed it, but Mr. Walker was not one of them. This made him wonder why the lavender smell was in the shop. Could it be a clue left behind by the thief, or was it just meant to distract him?

Danny considered both possibilities carefully. He knew that every detail could be important in solving the case, so he didn't want to ignore anything that might be useful. The presence of lavender seemed too specific to overlook, so he decided to keep it in mind.

To make sure he remembered everything, Danny took out his detective journal and wrote down his observations. He noted the lavender scent and his thoughts about its potential significance. By recording this detail, he ensured that he wouldn't forget it and could refer back to it later as he continued his investigation.

Next, Danny carefully looked at the area where the necklace had been displayed. To his surprise, he found a tiny, glimmering bead that was partly hidden in a corner. The bead caught the light and sparkled, drawing his attention immediately.

Danny's heart began to race with excitement.He wondered if this small bead could be a part of the missing necklace that was accidentally dropped during the robbery. The discovery felt significant, and he hoped it might be a crucial piece of evidence in solving the case.

Danny gently picked up the bead using a pair of tweezers to avoid touching it with his fingers. He then placed the bead under his magnifying lens for a closer look. The magnifying lens allowed him to see every detail of the bead more clearly.

After examining it carefully, Danny felt confident that the bead was definitely a part of the stolen necklace. The design and details matched what he had seen in the pictures of the missing jewelry. This discovery made him even more determined to solve the case and find the rest of the necklace.

As Danny's mind raced with theories,he mentally retraced the thief's steps. He tried to imagine what might have happened during the robbery and how the thief had moved through the shop. The lavender scent suggested that someone who liked that smell might be involved, but the bead brought up new questions.

Danny wondered why the bead was left behind and how it ended up in the corner where he found it. He thought about whether it had been dropped by mistake or if it had a different significance. These questions made him even more curious and determined to figure out what had really happened.

With many thoughts and ideas spinning in his mind, Danny decided to seek advice from someone he trusted deeply—his grandfather. His grandfather was a retired detective whose wisdom and experience had always been a source of guidance for Danny in his own investigations. Danny knew that his grandfather's insights could help him make sense of the clues and challenges he was facing.

Danny arrived at his grandfather's cozy cottage,where he was warmly greeted with a comforting smile and a big hug. The cottage had a welcoming feel, which made Danny feel at ease as he prepared to share his concerns. He appreciated the warmth and support his grandfather always offered.

of the missing necklace.With his grandfather's wisdom echoing in his mind, he was ready to face whatever challenges lay ahead on this thrilling adventure.

Sitting down with his grandfather, Danny eagerly explained the situation. He talked about the clues he had found, including the lavender scent and the tiny bead. He also shared his theories and thoughts about what these clues might mean. His grandfather listened carefully, ready to offer his valuable advice and help Danny solve the mystery.

His grandfather listened carefully, nodding as Danny spoke. He paid close attention to every detail Danny shared, showing that he was fully engaged in the discussion. As Danny finished explaining, his grandfather gave him a reassuring pat on the shoulder.

"You are on the right track, Danny," he said with a warm smile. His words were meant to encourage and support his grandson. He was pleased with Danny's progress and wanted him to know that he was making good headway in the investigation.

"Lavender could indeed be an important clue," his grandfather continued, his voice thoughtful. "But remember, in a case like this, every detail matters." He emphasized the importance of paying attention to all the small pieces of evidence, as they could be crucial in solving the mystery.

He continued, "The thief could have left the bead behind either on purpose or by accident. It's important to consider both possibilities as you try to solve the case." His grandfather's suggestion was meant to help Danny explore all angles of the situation.

"To figure this out," he said, "try to think like the thief. Imagine why the thief might have wanted to leave a clue behind. Consider their possible reasons and what they might have been trying to communicate." He also advised Danny to think about what the bead might reveal about the thief's actions and intentions.

Danny listened closely to his grandfather's advice, feeling grateful for the helpful guidance. He took in every word and knew that this advice would be important for solving the case. His grandfather's insights gave him a new perspective on the clues.

As he considered the possibilities, Danny spoke out loud, "Maybe the thief left the bead on purpose to mislead us." He thought that the thief might have intended to confuse him and make the investigation more challenging . "Or," Danny continued, "perhaps the thief was rushing and accidentally dropped the bead." He saw this as another potential explanation for why the bead was left behind.

With new ideas and a renewed sense of purpose, Danny went back to the jewelry shop. He was more determined than ever to find the missing necklace. He knew that with his grandfather's advice in mind, he might uncover something important.

Danny carefully examined every part of the shop again, paying close attention to details he might have missed before. He checked every corner and surface, looking for additional clues that could help solve the case. His thorough search reflected his commitment to finding the truth and solving the mystery.

As the sun started to set and the sky grew darker, Danny's excitement increased. He began to find more subtle clues that seemed to hint at who the thief might be and why they had stolen the necklace. Although the mystery was still not completely solved, these new clues made him feel like he was getting closer to understanding what had happened.

With his grandfather's wise advice still fresh in his mind, Danny felt more prepared than ever. He knew that he was one step closer to solving the mystery of the missing necklace. As he continued his investigation, he was ready to tackle any new challenges that came his way, eager to uncover the truth and complete this thrilling adventure.

Chapter 3: Rallying Support

News quickly spread throughout Midrock that Detective Danny was making significant progress in finding the missing necklace. Everyone in the town, both young and old, heard about Danny's efforts and were filled with admiration and hope for the young detective.

The residents believed in Danny's abilities and knew he had the skills to solve this tricky mystery. They felt confident that if anyone could uncover the truth and find the necklace, it was Danny. Their support and faith in him motivated Danny even more to succeed in his mission.

As Danny continued his investigation, the support from the community grew stronger every day. People in the town began to rally around him, offering their help and encouragement. Friends and classmates eagerly joined in, wanting to assist in any way possible.

Even some curious adults in the town stepped forward to offer their support. They admired Danny's dedication and passion for finding the truth. The community's eagerness to lend a hand showed how much they believed in him and wanted to see him succeed in solving the mystery.

Even the local shop owners got involved by putting up posters around town. The posters had a picture of the stolen necklace and contact information for anyone who might have a lead. These posters were displayed in shop windows, on bulletin boards, and in other prominent places to make sure everyone saw them.

Shopkeepers who had been working on the night of the theft also came forward with helpful information. They shared any unusual things they had seen or heard, providing valuable clues. Their contributions were important in helping Danny piece together what had happened and get closer to solving the mystery.

The way the town came together to help Danny was truly heartwarming. Seeing everyone's support and encouragement gave him a boost of motivation. He felt inspired to work even harder on solving the mystery.

Danny knew he couldn't let down all the people who believed in him, especially Mr. Walker. Mr. Walker's hope for getting his precious necklace back depended on Danny's efforts. This made Danny even more determined to push forward and succeed in his mission.

Danny's best friend, Katy, was right by his side throughout the investigation. She had always supported him in his detective adventures, and her constant presence was a great comfort. Katy's insatiable curiosity made her the perfect partner for Danny, as they both shared a deep passion for solving mysteries.

Katy's brilliant ideas often complemented Danny's sharp observations. Her enthusiasm and creative thinking helped to enhance their investigation. Together, they made a strong team, combining their skills to tackle the case and get closer to finding the missing necklace.

One afternoon, Danny and Katy were sitting on a bench in the park, going through the clues they had collected so far. They carefully reviewed each piece of information, discussing their findings and trying to understand how everything fit together. The park was peaceful, providing a quiet space for them to think.

As they talked, they exchanged theories and bounced ideas off each other. They worked together to make sense of the mystery they were trying to solve. Their conversations were filled with enthusiasm and determination, as they aimed to piece together the puzzle and get closer to solving the case.

Katy looked at Danny with admiration in her eyes. "You're doing great, Danny," she said warmly. "I'm sure we'll find that necklace soon."

Danny smiled, feeling grateful for Katy's steadfast support. "Thanks, Katy," he replied. "With your help and the support from everyone in town, I'm confident we'll solve this case."

As the sun set and the sky darkened , the park was illuminated by the soft glow of streetlights. The evening atmosphere was calm and peaceful, making it a perfect time for a short break. Danny and Katy decided it was a good moment to step away from their investigation.

They headed to Mr. Walker's charming little cafe to enjoy a slice of his famous apple pie. The cafe was cozy and welcoming, and the pie was a delightful treat that gave them a chance to relax and recharge before continuing their work.

As Danny and Katy enjoyed their time in the cozy cafe, they noticed the lively chatter among the other customers. The townspeople were excitedly discussing Detective Danny and his determination to catch the thief. The atmosphere in the cafe was filled with energy and enthusiasm.

Danny and Katy could hear people praising Danny's hard work and dedication. The support from the townspeople was clear, as many were cheering him on and expressing their belief in his ability to solve the case. This encouragement made Danny feel even more motivated to continue his investigation.

Mr. Walker, busy serving his customers in the cafe, looked over at Danny and Katy from time to time. Despite his busy schedule, he made sure to catch their attention and give them a warm smile. His expression showed how much he appreciated their hard work.

Mr. Walker felt grateful for Danny and Katy's dedication to solving the mystery. The case had deeply affected him, and their efforts gave him hope. He was thankful for their commitment and felt encouraged by their determination to find the missing necklace.

"Mr. Walker believes in us, " Katy said softly, a determined gleam in his eyes. "We won't let him down.
Danny nodded, his resolve strengthening with every passing moment. "You're right, Katy. We won't stop until we find that necklace and bring it back to him."

With renewed determination and the strong support from their town, Danny and Katy felt reassured that they were not alone in their mission. The encouragement from the community gave them confidence and strengthened their resolve. They knew that everyone was rooting for them as they worked to solve the mystery of the missing necklace.

Together, Danny and Katy were prepared to tackle any challenges that came their way. They felt optimistic that justice would be served and that the missing necklace would soon be returned to its rightful owner. Their shared commitment and the town's support made them believe that they would succeed in their quest.

Chapter 4: A Twist at Twilight

Danny visited the only florist in town, Mr. Higgins, who was known for his gentle nature and deep love for plants. Mr. Higgins had a reputation for being wise and knowledgeable about flowers and greenery. As Danny walked into the flower shop, Mr. Higgins greeted him with a warm and friendly smile.

"Ah,Detective Danny," Mr. Higgins said in a kind voice, recognizing the young detective right away. "How can I assist you today?" His welcoming tone and genuine interest made Danny feel comfortable as he prepared to ask for help with his investigation.

Danny explained to Mr. Higgins that he had found a lavender scent at the crime scene and asked if he had sold any lavender recently. He was hoping that the information might help him in his investigation. Mr. Higgins took a moment to think about the question before responding.

"Yes," Mr. Higgins said thoughtfully, "I did sell a bunch of lavender to a gentleman a few days ago." He recalled that the man had seemed quite rushed and had mentioned he was planning a surprise for someone special. This detail might be important, and Danny made a note of it for further investigation.

Danny's detective instincts were immediately on high alert.He quickly asked Mr. Higgins for a description of the man who had bought the lavender. Mr. Higgins described him as a tall and mysterious figure who wore a long coat and had his hat pulled low over his face.

"That's definitely a lead worth following up on," Danny said, feeling more focused on his investigation. He thanked Mr. Higgins for his help, knowing that this new information could be crucial in solving the case.

"That's definitely a lead worth following up on," Danny said , feeling more focused on his investigation. He thanked

Mr. Higgins for his help, knowing that this new information could be crucial in solving the case.

As the sun began to set and the sky turned darker, Danny's mind was filled with different possibilities. He thought about the mysterious man who had bought the lavender and wondered why he had done so before the theft. Danny realized that there must have been a reason for this purchase.

He started to think that the lavender might have been used to hide the thief's scent. If the thief had used it to cover up their smell, it could have been a way to confuse any tracking dogs that might have been used to follow their trail. This idea seemed to make sense and gave Danny a new direction for his investigation.

Danny decided to tell Katy about the new clue he had discovered. They agreed to head over to Mr. Walker's shop together to share the information. As they walked towards the shop, they noticed that there was a lot of excitement near the town square.

A small crowd had gathered around a local newsstand, and their animated voices drew Danny's attention. Curious about what was causing the commotion, he and Katy approached the newsstand to find out what was happening.

"What's going on?" Katy wondered aloud.

Danny approached the newsstand and saw a headline that read, "Young Detective Danny's Race Against Time."

The town had come together to support Danny, and now his investigation was the main topic of conversation. The local newspaper had published an article about his work, highlighting his progress, his determination, and the strong support he was receiving from the community.

As Danny read the article, he felt a mix of pride and responsibility. It was clear that everyone in Midrock was watching his every move. The attention made him even more determined to solve the case and live up to the trust the town had placed in him.

With renewed determination, Danny and Katy went back to work inside Mr. Walker's shop. They were ready to continue their investigation with fresh energy and focus. The shop felt different from before the theft; there was a noticeable sense of loss and sadness in the air, making the atmosphere heavier.

Despite the somber mood, there was still a sense of hope in the shop. Danny and Katy could feel that the community's support and their own determination brought a glimmer of optimism. They were committed to finding the missing necklace and restoring a sense of normalcy and joy to Mr. Walker and the town.

As Danny and Katy carefully examined the scene, Danny spotted something unusual. There was a faint scratch mark on the window ledge that was barely noticeable. He pointed it out to Katy, and they both took a closer look.

They discussed the mark and thought it might have been left by the thief when they either entered or exited the shop. The tiny scratch could be a crucial clue, and Danny and Katy knew they needed to investigate it further to understand its significance in solving the case.

With this new clue in hand, Danny and Katy decided to ask the neighboring shopkeepers if they had noticed anything unusual around the time of the theft. They were hoping that someone might have seen or heard something that could help their investigation.

Mr. Wilson, who ran the bakery next door, remembered hearing a faint noise on the night of the theft. He wasn't sure what it was, but it caught his attention. This piece of information could be important, so Danny and Katy made a note of it and planned to follow up on this lead.

was determined to bring "The Mystery of the Missing Necklace" to a close and restore the precious necklace to its rightful owner, Mr. Walker.

"I was in my kitchen, baking bread," Mr. Wilson explained. "While I was working, I heard a soft tapping sound. It was like someone was trying to open a window." He remembered the sound clearly, even though it was faint.

Hearing this , Danny felt a rush of excitement. The combination of the scratch mark on the window ledge and Mr. Wilson's description of the tapping noise suggested that the thief might have used the window to get into the shop. This new information gave Danny and Katy a promising lead to investigate further.

As the evening fell over Midrock and the sky grew darker, Detective Danny and Katy began to feel hopeful. They were excited because they were getting closer to solving the mystery. The clues they had gathered, including the mysterious man who bought lavender from Mr. Higgins, the faint scratch mark on the window ledge, and the tapping noise that Mr. Wilson had heard, were starting to come together.

These pieces of information were beginning to fit together like parts of a jigsaw puzzle. Danny and Katy could see how the clues were related, and it gave them confidence that they were on the right track. Their investigation was making progress, and they were more determined than ever to find the missing necklace.

But the biggest question still loomed: who was the mysterious man, and what was his connection to the stolen necklace? Danny knew that solving this question was key to cracking the case. As the darkness settled over the town, he felt a sense of urgency. The answer to this mystery seemed to be just out of reach, but Danny was determined to find it.

With the support of the entire town of Midrock behind him, Danny felt more motivated than ever. The community's encouragement gave him strength, and his own determination was unwavering. He knew that the next crucial breakthrough in the case might be just around the corner.

As night fell , Danny was prepared to face whatever challenges came his way. He was ready to continue his relentless pursuit of justice. The young detective was committed to solving "The Mystery of the Missing Necklace" and returning the precious item to its rightful owner, Mr. Walker.

Night had fallen, and Detective Danny and Katy pressed on with their investigation under the cover of darkness. The quiet streets and dimly lit corners added a sense of mystery to their pursuit, making the case feel even more urgent.

The town of Midrock seemed eerily silent, almost as if it was holding its breath, waiting for a resolution to the puzzling case. The stillness of the night heightened Danny and Katy's determination to uncover the truth and solve the mystery once and for all.

As they walked back from the jewelry shop, Danny kept thinking about the mysterious man who had bought lavender from Mr. Higgins. This man's actions seemed innocent on the surface, but Danny was convinced there was more to the story.

The purchase of the lavender couldn't be a simple coincidence, and Danny was determined to uncover the reason behind it. He knew that finding out why the man had bought thc lavender might be the key to solving the case, and he was resolved to get to the bottom of it.

Their next lead directed them to the outskirts of town, where a circus had set up its colorful tents. The circus coming to

Midrock was an annual event that everyone looked forward to, bringing excitement and wonder to the town. Normally, the circus was a place of joy and laughter, filled with the sounds of cheerful music and delighted children.

However, tonight the circus grounds felt different. As Danny and Katy walked through the dimly lit paths, the usual lively atmosphere was replaced by an eerie silence. The shadows cast by the tents seemed to hold secrets, and the young detectives felt a sense of urgency as they searched for clues. The familiar place now felt mysterious, adding another layer of intrigue to their investigation.

As they neared the main tent , the sounds of laughter and lively music filled the air. The circus performers were busy rehearsing their acts, each practicing their unique skills with enthusiasm. The joyful noises created a stark contrast to the quiet, eerie paths they had just walked through.

Colorful lights illuminated the night sky, casting a cheerful glow over the circus grounds. The bright lights and vibrant atmosphere made it feel as if the circus was in full swing, even though it was just a rehearsal. Despite the festive scene, Danny and Katy remained focused on their mission, determined to find any clues related to the missing necklace.

Danny noticed a man standing near the entrance, watching the performers with keen interest. There was something about him that seemed familiar to Danny, and he couldn't shake the feeling that he had seen this man before. The way the man observed the acts, with a sharp and focused gaze, made Danny's intuition kick in.

"Could this be the mysterious man who had purchased the lavender?", Danny wondered. The pieces of the puzzle seemed to be coming together, and he felt a surge of excitement. He knew they had to approach the man and find out more. Danny whispered to Katy, pointing subtly towards the man, and they both prepared to make their move.

As Danny and Katy approached, the man noticed them and turned his gaze their way. His eyes were sharp and intense, giving off the feeling that he knew something important. He was dressed in a long coat, and his hat was pulled down low, almost hiding his face. A sly, mischievous smile was visible on his lips, adding to his mysterious appearance.

"Can I help you?" the man asked, his voice carrying a hint of curiosity. His demeanor made it clear that he was intrigued by their presence, and Danny and Katy knew they would need to be careful with their next words.

Detective Danny took a deep breath and introduced himself to the man. He explained that he was working on a case involving the disappearance of a valuable necklace from Mr. Walker's jewelry shop. Danny made sure to mention the importance of the necklace and how it had gone missing.

He detailed how the theft was a significant concern for both Mr. Walker and the entire town of Midrock. Danny hoped that by sharing this information, the man might provide useful details that could help solve the mystery and recover the precious necklace.

The man's smile slowly faded, and for a brief moment, his eyes shifted away as if he was caught off guard. Then, he looked directly at Danny with a mix of curiosity and amusement.

"Ah, Detective Danny, how intriguing," he said with a hint of amusement in his voice. "What brings you to our humble circus tonight?" His tone was casual, but there was an underlying tension, as if he was both interested and cautious about Danny's presence.

Danny chose to be straightforward with the man. "We have a reason to think that you might know something about the missing necklace ," he said firmly. "You purchased lavender from Mr. Higgins recently, and we need to understand how that might be related to the case."

Danny made it clear that the lavender purchase was a significant clue in their investigation. He hoped that by being direct, the man would provide information that could help solve the mystery and lead them closer to finding the missing necklace.

The man's eyes narrowed, but he remained composed. "Ah, the lavender, " he mused. "A lovely scent, isn't it? But what does it have to do with the necklace?"

Detective Danny didn't let the man's vague response throw him off. He pressed on with his investigation. "We discovered traces of lavender at the scene where the necklace was stolen," Danny explained firmly. "This could be a clue left behind by the thief."

Danny's tone was serious as he spoke, making it clear that the lavender was a significant lead in the case. He hoped this would encourage the man to provide more information or clarify his involvement in the mystery.

The man's expression changed slightly, and Danny could tell he was making progress.He felt confident that he was getting closer to something important. Just as Danny was about to ask more questions, a deep voice cut through the conversation.

"What's going on here?" the voice asked, breaking the tension. The interruption was sudden, and Danny turned to see who had spoken, ready to address the new presence and continue his investigation.

A large , burly man dressed in a ringmaster's outfit approached the group. His commanding presence made it clear that he was someone important, and his eyes were filled with suspicion as they scanned Danny and Katy.

"We were just having a friendly chat," the mysterious man said, throwing a quick glance at Danny. His tone was casual, but there was an underlying edge to his words, suggesting that he was wary of the young detective's presence.

The ringmaster looked Danny up and down, studying him with a critical eye. "This is a private area," he said firmly. His tone left no room for doubt that he was serious about keeping the space exclusive.

"We don't appreciate uninvited guests wandering around," he continued , making it clear that Danny and Katy were not welcome. His stern demeanor emphasized his authority and his desire to keep the investigation away from the circus grounds.

Danny stayed calm and collected in response to the ringmaster's stern words. "I apologize for the intrusion," he said politely. "We didn't mean to cause any trouble."

He continued with a respectful tone , explaining their purpose. "We are simply trying to find some information that could help us solve an important case. We are not here to interfere, just to gather clues that might assist in our investigation."

As the ringmaster walked off, the mysterious man turned his attention back to Danny and Katy. There was a hint of curiosity in his eyes as he looked at them. "You've certainly caught my interest, Detective Danny," he said, his voice carrying a note of intrigue.

"But I need to warn you," he continued, leaning in slightly, "the circus can be a tricky and dangerous place. Be cautious about what you find out. Not everything here is as it seems."

With the mysterious warning given, the man vanished into the shadows of the circus grounds. Danny and Katy looked at each other , both feeling more curious than ever. The man's words and his sudden disappearance only made them more determined to uncover the truth.

As they walked back to town, Danny couldn't stop thinking about their encounter at the circus. He felt strongly that the circus might be key to solving the case. There seemed to be a connection between the mysterious man, the lavender, and the missing necklace, but Danny still needed to figure out how they all fit together.

The circus had added a new layer of complexity to the case, making the mystery even more intriguing and dangerous. Danny felt that the vibrant world of the circus was now a crucial part of the puzzle. As he looked up at the twinkling stars above, he realized that the answers he was searching for might be hidden somewhere in the midst of the circus's lively atmosphere.

Determined to uncover the truth , Danny was prepared to face any challenges that came his way. With Katy by his side and the support of the town behind him, he was ready for whatever twists the circus had in store. This thrilling adventure of "The Mystery of the Missing Necklace" was far from over, and Danny was more committed than ever to solving it.

The next morning, as the sun rose over Midrock, Detective Danny and Katy met at Mr. Walker's jewelry shop. They were eager to discuss what they had discovered during their visit to the circus. The mysterious man's link to the missing necklace was still unclear, and they realized they needed more clues to solve the case.

Danny knew they couldn't give up. They needed to dig deeper and find out more about the mysterious man and his connection to the theft. With determination in their hearts, they planned their next steps, knowing that every piece of information brought them closer to solving the mystery.

"I think we should dig deeper into the history of the necklace" Danny suggested. "Maybe there's something in its past that could give us a clue about the thief's motives."

Katy nodded in agreement. "That's a great idea, Danny. Mr. Walker mentioned that the necklace held sentimental value to him. Lct's see if there's any historical information about it that might help us."

With their plan in mind, Danny and Katy made their way to the town's historical library. The library was located in a beautiful old building, its walls lined with dusty bookshelves filled with stories from the past. It was a place where secrets and knowledge lay waiting to be discovered.

As they stepped inside, the quiet atmosphere and the scent of old books welcomed them. Danny and Katy knew that the information they needed might be hidden somewhere in those shelves, and they were ready to dive into the library's vast collection to uncover any clues that could help solve the mystery of the missing necklace.

As they entered the library, they were greeted warmly by the librarian, Mrs. Jenkins. She was a kind woman with glasses perched on her nose and a welcoming smile. "Ah, Detective Danny and Katy!" she exclaimed, recognizing the young sleuths immediately.

"What brings you here today?" Mrs. Jenkins asked with genuine curiosity. She knew they must be on the trail of something important, given their determined expressions.

"We're trying to learn more about a valuable necklace that went missing, " Danny replied. "Do you have any records on historical jewelry in Midrock?"

Mrs. Jenkins nodded and guided them to a section filled with books about the town's rich history. The shelves were lined with dusty tomes, each holding stories from the past.

Among the books, they found one titled "Jewels of Midrock: Treasures Through the Ages." The title seemed promising, and they felt a surge of excitement as they pulled it from the shelf, hoping it might contain clues about the missing necklace.

With the book in hand, they settled at a table and began flipping through its pages. The worn pages revealed the history of numerous famous jewelry pieces that had been worn by the people of Midrock over the centuries.

As they read , they found fascinating stories about the origins, craftsmanship, and significance of each piece. They hoped to uncover any mention of the missing necklace or clues that could lead them closer to solving the case.

As they continued reading, a particular passage grabbed Danny's attention. It was titled "The Rose of Midrock: A Necklace of Legendary Beauty." The passage detailed a necklace created centuries ago, famous for its stunning design and mythical origins.

Danny's excitement grew as he read about the necklace's intricate craftsmanship and the legends surrounding it. This seemed to match the description of the missing necklace, and he hoped that this information would help him in solving the case.

Intrigued, Danny continued reading. The passage explained that the necklace had been handed down through many generations, with each new owner adding their own special touch to its beauty. It was described as a treasured heirloom with a rich history.

According to the book, the necklace was believed to have mystical powers. It was said to bring good fortune and blessings to whoever owned it. This added layer of mystery and significance made the necklace even more valuable and intriguing.

"The Rose of Midrock," Danny whispered."Could this be the same necklace that Mr. Walker crafted?"

Katy's eyes widened with excitement. "It's possible, Danny! This could explain its sentimental value to him. But what does it have to do with the thief?"

Danny furrowed his brow, deep in thought. "If the necklace indeed holds mystical powers, it might have caught the attention of someone who desires its magic, " he reasoned. "But why would they steal it? And why leave behind the clues?"

While Danny and Katy were deep in thought, Mrs. Jenkins came over to their table carrying a stack of old newspapers. She placed the papers gently in front of them and smiled warmly.

"I thought these might be useful for your investigation, "Mrs. Jenkins said. She had noticed their intense focus and wanted to offer additional resources that could help them uncover more information.

The stack of newspapers was filled with articles from years past, showcasing various jewel heists and historical crimes. Danny and Katy carefully flipped through them, looking for anything relevant to their current investigation.

One particular headline drew Danny's attention.It read,"The Rose of Midrock: A History of Thefts." Intrigued, Danny focused on this article, hoping it might reveal more about the legendary necklace and any past incidents involving it.

The article provided an intriguing account of several thefts involving The Rose of Midrock necklace throughout history. It described how, due to the necklace's legendary status and the belief in its magical powers, it had been a prime target for thieves over the centuries.

Each theft was depicted as a bold attempt by criminals drawn to the necklace's reputed enchantments. The article suggested that its allure had consistently attracted those hoping to claim its rumored powers for themselves.

Katy gasped. "So, the necklace has a history of being stolen, and it's happening again!"

Danny nodded,feeling a puzzle piece fall into place."Exactly. And it looks like the mysterious man might be aware of the necklace's history too."

As Danny and Katy continued reading the articles,they discovered that each theft of The Rose of Midrock had been shrouded in mystery. The articles described how investigators were often left puzzled by strange clues that seemed to lead nowhere.

Some reports even suggested that the necklace had a kind of protective power. According to these claims, the necklace might somehow shield itself from those with bad intentions , making it difficult for thieves to find and steal it. This idea added a new layer of intrigue to their investigation.

With this new information, Danny began to understand that The Rose of Midrock was far more complex than he had first thought. The necklace's history was not just about its beauty but also involved a long series of mysterious thefts and legends about its powers.

Danny knew that the current case was deeply connected to the necklace's past. This realization gave him a renewed sense of purpose. He was now more determined than ever to uncover the truth behind The Rose of Midrock and solve the mystery surrounding it.

As they walked out of the library , Danny and Katy felt a surge of excitement. They had uncovered valuable historical details that were bringing them closer to solving "The Mystery of the Missing Necklace." With the new information about the necklace's past and its legendary importance, Danny and Katy felt they were making real progress.

Danny and Katy were eager to move forward with their investigation. They were now prepared for the next steps in their adventure, determined to piece together all the clues they had gathered and solve the mystery. With each new discovery, they felt more confident that they would soon find the missing necklace.

The clues were slowly falling into place, and with each new piece of information, Danny's excitement grew stronger. He could feel that the solution to the mystery was getting closer and closer. Every revelation brought him one step nearer to solving the case.

Danny realized that finding the truth would lead him deep into Midrock's history. The secrets of The Rose of Midrock necklace were hidden in the town's past, and he was determined to uncover them. He knew that understanding this rich history was key to solving the case and achieving justice.

Chapter 7: The Hidden Message

With their new understanding of The Rose of Midrock necklace's history, Detective Danny and Katy pressed on with their investigation. They knew that they were dealing with a mystery that had captivated people for centuries, and this knowledge added both excitement and pressure to their task.

As they moved into the next phase of their adventure, they felt the weight of the necklace's long history of intrigue and mystery. Each step they took in their investigation felt more significant, as if they were uncovering secrets that had been hidden for ages.

Their first destination was Mr. Walker's jewelry shop, where they hoped to confirm whether the necklace he had crafted was truly "The Rose of Midrock." Danny and Katy wanted to verify if the piece they were investigating was connected to the legendary necklace mentioned in the historical records.

Upon arriving at the shop, they approached Mr. Walker with their new findings. They explained the legendary history of The Rose of Midrock and discussed the necklace's connections to past thefts. Danny and Katy hoped this would help clarify if Mr. Walker's necklace was indeed the same one tied to so many historical mysteries.

Mr. Walker's eyes grew wide with surprise as he listened to the story Danny and Katy shared. "I had no idea," he whispered, his voice filled with awe. He was clearly moved by the revelation.

"I knew the necklace was special," Mr. Walker continued, "but I never imagined it was connected to such a legendary past." His amazement reflected how unexpected and significant the discovery was for him.

"That's the question we're trying to answer, " Danny replied. "The clues and the mysterious man's actions indicate that he might be aware of the necklace's history and its supposed powers."

With Mr. Walker's support and approval, Danny and Katy felt more determined than ever to pursue every lead in their investigation. They knew they were getting closer to solving the mystery and were ready to follow each clue thoroughly.

Their next lead took them back to the circus, where they hoped to find more answers. With renewed energy and focus, they prepared to dig deeper into the circus's secrets to uncover the truth behind the missing necklace.

When Danny and Katy arrived at the circus grounds, they immediately sensed a change in the atmosphere. The usual lively energy was still there, with performers getting ready for the evening's show. However, there was a new feeling of tension and secrecy hanging in the air that Danny couldn't ignore.

The performers moved with a sense of urgency and quiet , and the once cheerful circus environment now felt charged with an underlying tension. Danny and Katy exchanged looks, aware that something was different and that this change might be connected to their investigation.

Danny and Katy walked up to the ringmaster , hoping to learn more about the mysterious man they had seen at the circus. The ringmaster seemed unsure and a bit wary at first, but they managed to persuade him by mentioning their investigation into the missing necklace.

After a bit of convincing, the ringmaster agreed to help them. Although he was still cautious, he was willing to share what he knew in the hopes of resolving the situation.

"He goes by the name of Marcel, "the ringmaster revealed. "He joined our circus just a few days ago, claiming to be a magician. But there's something odd about him."

"Marcel," Danny repeated,making a mental note of the name. "Did he give any reason for joining the circus?" The ringmaster shrugged."He said he was looking for a new opportunity to showcase his talents. But I can't shake the feeling that he's hiding something."

With this new information, Danny and Katy decided to dig deeper into Marcel's activities. They found out that Marcel had been spotted acting suspiciously around the circus. He had been seen sneaking around different areas, such as the performers' tents and the animal cages.

It seemed that Marcel was trying to stay out of sight while exploring these places. His secretive behavior raised more questions, and Danny and Katy were determined to uncover what he was looking for and how it related to the missing necklace.

The next morning, as Detective Danny was leaving his house, he noticed a letter on his doorstep. Curious, he picked it up and opened it. Inside, he found a drawing of an emblem featuring a moon embracing a necklace. Danny quickly realized that this symbol might be a clue leading him to the necklace's location.

Danny met up with Katy and showed her the letter. Together, they examined the emblem, trying to figure out what it might mean. Despite their efforts, Katy couldn't make sense of the symbol, and the mystery of the moon and necklace remained unsolved.

With the riddle in hand, Danny and Katy felt a surge of determination. They were excited to solve the puzzle, believing that this message held the key to finding the missing necklace. They knew that if they could crack the code, they would be one step closer to solving the mystery.

As they studied the riddle , their minds raced with possibilities. They were confident that the answer to the mystery was hidden in the message , just waiting to be uncovered. Danny and Katy were ready to put all their effort into solving this new challenge and continuing their search for the necklace.

As the sun began to set, casting an amber glow over the circus grounds, Detective Danny and Katy stood at the cusp of a breakthrough. The riddle held the key to the necklace's whereabouts, and with every moment that passed, they felt closer to unraveling the centuries-old mystery.

The adventure of "The Hidden Message" had led them to this crucial moment, where everything they had learned and experienced would be put to the test. Danny knew that their skills, clever thinking, and bravery were about to face their biggest challenge yet.

With Katy by his side and the strong support of the town backing them, Danny felt more determined than ever. He believed that the answers they had been searching for were very close, and he was ready to uncover the truth.

As Danny and Katy stood in front of the mysterious riddle, they felt a rush of excitement and anticipation. Their hard work and investigations had brought them to this key moment, and they were eager to see what they would uncover.

They knew that solving this riddle was crucial to finding the truth about the missing necklace. The legend of The Rose of Midrock had been shrouded in mystery for a long time, and they were determined to reveal its secrets and bring its story to light once again.

Chapter 8: Perilous Pursuit

With the riddle in hand, Detective Danny and Katy began their dangerous quest to understand its hidden message. As the sun set, casting long shadows over the circus grounds, they felt a sense of urgency and excitement.

They found themselves drawn to a place where stars and shadows came together – the center of the circus ring. This spot seemed to hold a special significance, and they hoped it would reveal the secrets they were searching for.

"The riddle mentions 'the moon's embrace.' Maybe it refers to the night sky", Katy suggested, looking up at the darkening canopy above.

Danny nodded, his mind racing with possibilities. "And the necklace glowing in moonlight could mean that the location is somehow illuminated or revealed by the moon."

They started to closely examine the area , looking for anything that matched the description in the riddle. The circus ring, which was usually full of life and color, felt strangely quiet under the night sky.

As they walked around the ring, Danny spotted something shining in one corner. His heart raced with anticipation, and he signaled Katy to come over and take a closer look.

"There!" he exclaimed, pointing to a small, silver emblem embedded in the ground.

Katy crouched down and brushed away the dirt to reveal an intricate design etched into the emblem . It resembled a crescent moon surrounded by stars. "This must be it!" she said excitedly. "The emblem represents the ' moon's embrace.' "

Danny's heart raced with anticipation. "Now, we just need to find where the necklace could be hidden within this ring."

As they continued their investigation,Danny spotted a series of faint markings on the ground. These markings formed a path that led away from the emblem, winding its way around the circus ring.

It seemed as though someone had carefully traced a pattern, leaving a trail for them to follow. Danny pointed out the markings to Katy, and together, they decided to follow the path, hoping it would lead them closer to solving the mystery.

Following the path, they eventually reached the edge of the circus grounds. Here, a row of large, majestic oak trees stood tall, their branches creating a thick canopy overhead.

The markings guided them to one specific oak tree, which seemed even grander than the rest. Its branches stretched out wide, almost as if they were protecting something hidden beneath. Danny and Katy exchanged hopeful glances, sensing that they were on the verge of a significant discovery.

Danny's eyes gleamed with excitement. "This must be the 'necklace glowing in moonlight.' The tree's branches could be the necklace."

Katy looked up at the tree and noticed that one of its branches seemed different from the others. Unlike the rest, this branch had something wrapped around it.

In the soft glow of the moonlight, she saw a faint glimmer , but enough to catch her eye. She pointed it out to Danny, and they both felt a surge of excitement. They knew they were close to uncovering something important.

Danny and Katy climbed up to the branch to get a closer look. As they reached it, they discovered a shimmering silver thread woven delicately into the tree's bark. The thread sparkled faintly in the moonlight, guiding their attention.

Following the thread , they found a small hidden compartment tucked away among the leaves. It was cleverly concealed, blending in with the tree's natural appearance. Their excitement grew as they realized this could be a significant clue in their investigation.

Danny and Katy held their breath as Danny carefully opened the hidden compartment. Inside, they found a beautifully ornate box, decorated with intricate carvings. The box looked old and special, catching their eye immediately.

As they gently lifted the box and opened it, a brilliant, radiant glow filled the night air. The soft light illuminated their faces, revealing the box's precious contents. This unexpected discovery filled them with excitement and hope that they were on the right track.

Inside the box, they found The Rose of Midrock necklace, and it was even more beautiful than they had imagined. The necklace was decorated with dazzling gems that sparkled like stars. Its intricate design was incredibly detailed and seemed to glow with a magical charm.

As they looked closer, the necklace's enchanting beauty became even clearer. The way the light caught the gems made the entire piece seem alive with a mesmerizing aura. It was clear that this was a treasure worth every bit of the legend surrounding it.

"It's breathtaking, " Katy whispered, her eyes wide with wonder.

Danny couldn't help but marvel at the necklace's beauty, but he knew their mission was not yet complete. They needed to find the mysterious man, Marcel, and uncover his true intentions.

As they made their way back to the circus grounds, Danny couldn't shake the feeling that Marcel was watching them. The eerie silence of the circus was now even more unsettling, and Danny's senses were on high alert.

Danny and Katy walked back to Marcel's tent,determined to confront him and uncover the truth about the theft. They hoped that by speaking with Marcel, they could finally solve the mystery.

As they neared the tent, they saw Marcel standing outside in the moonlight. His face was illuminated by the soft glow, and he wore a mysterious smile that seemed to hint at secrets yet to be revealed.

"So, you've found it, " Marcel said calmly, looking at the necklace in Danny's hand.
"Why did you steal it?" Danny asked, his voice firm. "What do you want with The Rose of Midrock?"
Marcel chuckled softly, a glimmer of both admiration and mischief dancing in his eyes. "You really are quite the detective, Danny," he said with a smile. "I knew you would manage to solve the riddle and find the necklace."

He paused for a moment, then continued with a hint of curiosity. "But do you honestly think this necklace has mystical powers? What do you believe it can actually do?"

Danny remained steadfast."I believe in the truth,"he replied. "And I'm determined to understand why you stole it."

Marcel's expression changed as he became more serious and thoughtful. "The Rose of Midrock isn't just a stunning piece of jewelry," he began, his voice filled with reflection. "According to legend, it has special powers. It's said to grant its wearer the ability to see the truth in any situation."

He continued, his tone revealing a hint of his own desire. "I wanted that power for myself. I thought if I could find the necklace, I could uncover hidden truths and see things clearly."

Danny's mind reeled with the revelation. "But what would you do with such a power?"

Marcel's eyes grew softer, revealing a hint of vulnerability. "I've dedicated much of my life to seeking answers and understanding the deeper mysteries of the world," he explained. "For a long time, I believed that The Rose of Midrock was the key to uncovering these hidden truths."

He continued, his voice filled with a mix of hope and regret. "I thought that if I could find the necklace, it would help me see and understand things that are usually hidden from view. It felt like the answer to many questions I've been searching to solve."

As Marcel spoke, Danny could hear a deep longing in his voice. It became clear that Marcel was not seeking the necklace out of greed, but rather out of a profound desire to uncover hidden truths.

Danny understood that Marcel's pursuit was about more than just possessing a valuable item. It was about a quest for knowledge and understanding, a drive to grasp the deeper secrets of the universe that had always eluded him.

"But stealing it wasn't the answer, " Katy interjected. "The necklace might have its own way of guiding those who seek it for the wrong reasons away from its true location."
Marcel nodded,a mix of regret and understanding on his face. "I see that now. I was blinded by my ambition, and I lost sight of what truly matters."

With the necklace safely returned to its rightful place, Danny and Katy knew their job wasn't finished yet. They realized that Marcel needed to face the consequences of his actions for trying to steal the necklace.

However, they also saw an opportunity for Marcel to make amends. They believed that if given a chance, he could redeem himself and perhaps find a way to use his quest for truth in a more positive way.

As the first light of dawn started to brighten the circus grounds, Danny knew it was time to make an important decision. He turned to Marcel and spoke with calm determination. "Marcel , you have a choice to make," Danny said firmly. "You can choose to turn yourself in for what you've done and face the consequences. Or, you can take a different path."

Danny continued, "Remember, the power to find the truth doesn't come from a necklace or any external source. It comes from within ourselves and how we choose to act. You have the chance to make things right and show that you've learned from this experience."

Marcel stood silently for a moment, looking deep in thought. It was clear that the reality of his past actions was hitting him hard. He seemed to be reflecting on the choices he had made and the consequences they brought. Finally, he spoke with a serious tone, "I will face the consequences of what I have done."

He then added, "But maybe there's still an opportunity for me to seek the truth in another way. I want to make amends and find a different path to understanding." Marcel's words showed a willingness to confront his mistakes and a desire to seek truth in a more meaningful manner.

With Marcel admitting his actions and the necklace safely returned to its rightful place, the mystery of "The Rose of Midrock" was finally resolved. The case that had captivated the town of Midrock had come to a satisfying end, and the precious necklace was now back where it belonged.

Detective Danny had not only solved the intricate puzzle but had also made a significant impact on Marcel. By understanding Marcel's true intentions and helping him face the consequences, Danny had touched the heart of someone who had been searching for something deeper than just a valuable artifact.

As they left the circus grounds, the town of Midrock welcomed the return of the precious necklace with great joy and relief. The streets were filled with celebrations as the people expressed their gratitude for having the beloved treasure back in their possession.

Detective Danny's reputation grew even stronger as a young detective with a heart of gold. The townspeople celebrated him as a hero, recognizing his dedication and skill in solving the mystery. Danny's success not only restored the necklace but also brought a sense of pride and unity to the entire town.

The Adventures of Detective Danny had come full circle, leading him through twists and turns, to the heart of a centuries-old legend.

Chapter 9: A Heartwarming Resolution

In the days after solving "The Mystery of the Missing Necklace," Midrock went back to its usual peaceful and lively state. The town resumed its normal rhythm, filled with the familiar sounds and sights that everyone enjoyed. The circus, having completed its run, packed up and left, but it left behind fond memories of the wonder and excitement it had brought to the town.

Mr. Walker's jewelry shop also returned to its happy bustle. The shop was filled with customers once again, all eager to see the beautiful creations displayed in the windows. The Rose of Midrock necklace was prominently featured , now carefully protected with extra security, ensuring its safety and preserving its place as a cherished treasure of the town.

Detective Danny and Katy kept going with their detective work, but now with a deep sense of satisfaction and happiness. They had faced many challenges together and their friendship had become even stronger through their experiences.

They both knew that, as a team, they were incredibly strong and capable. Their bond and trust in each other made them ready to tackle any new mysteries that came their way.

One afternoon, as the warm sun bathed Midrock in its golden glow, Danny and Katy sat on a park bench, reflecting on their journey.
"I can't believe how far we've come, " Katy said, smiling at Danny. "From solving small mysteries in the neighborhood to taking on a legendary case like The Rose of Midrock."

Danny grinned back, a spark of excitement in his eyes. "And it's all thanks to the support we had from everyone in Midrock, "he replied. "Their belief in us and the way the town rallied behind us gave us the strength to face any challenge."

Katy looked at Danny with a warm smile, clearly impressed by his achievements. "You really are an amazing detective,

Danny," she said, her voice full of pride. "And your kindness makes you even more special. You have a heart of gold."

At that moment, Mr. Walker came over, his face beaming with gratitude. "I can't express how grateful I am to both of you," he said sincerely. "You've not only returned The Rose of Midrock but also brought a renewed sense of hope and wonder to our town. Thank you so much."

Danny smiled warmly."It was a team effort , "he said humbly. "Without everyone's support, we wouldn't have been able to crack the case."

Mr. Walker's eyes sparkled with a playful glint. "Well, I do have a small token of appreciation for you, " he said, holding out a small box.

Curious, Danny opened the box to find a beautifully crafted detective badge, gleaming with gold and silver. "Wow, " he exclaimed, touched by the gesture. "Thank you, Mr. Walker."

"It's the least I can do,"he replied."You are now an official detective of Midrock, and you'll always have a special place in our hearts."

Mr. Walker's eyes sparkled with a playful glint."Well,I have a little something to show my appreciation," he said, presenting a small, neatly wrapped box.

Intrigued, Danny carefully opened the box and discovered a beautifully crafted detective badge, shining with both gold and silver. "Wow," Danny said, his voice filled with amazement and gratitude. "Thank you so much, Mr. Walker."

Danny carefully pinned the badge to his shirt, feeling a deep sense of pride and accomplishment. "I promise to wear it with honor," he said, his voice filled with sincerity.

As time passed and weeks went by , Danny and Katy continued their detective work with enthusiasm. But they didn't just focus on mysteries; they also made time for other activities. They enjoyed exploring new cases, having picnics in the park, and taking part in the town's annual talent show. Their lives were full of adventures and joyful moments, balancing their detective work with fun and friendship.

A few days later, Danny and Katy received a special invitation. The townspeople of Midrock had planned a gathering to honor them for their bravery and dedication in solving the mystery of The Rose of Midrock. It was a way for everyone to come together and celebrate the young detectives' hard work.

When the day of the celebration arrived, Danny and Katy were welcomed with open arms. They stood on a small stage set up in the town square, surrounded by a crowd of smiling faces. Friends, family, and the residents of Midrock all gathered to show their appreciation.

As Danny and Katy looked out at the sea of happy, grateful faces, they felt a deep sense of accomplishment. The celebration was a heartfelt tribute to their efforts, and it made them realize just how much their work had touched the lives of those around them.

The mayor of Midrock stepped forward."On behalf of the town, I present you with these medals of honor, " he said, placing gleaming medals around Danny and Katy's necks. "You are true heroes, and Midrock will forever be grateful for your courage and determination."

The crowd erupted in applause, and Danny and Katy were overwhelmed with emotions. They felt a surge of pride and happiness as they looked out at the cheering faces. The warmth and love from the town made them realize how much their detective adventures had meant to everyone.

As they stood there , soaking in the moment, Danny and Katy knew that their efforts had touched the hearts of many people. Their hard work and dedication had brought the community together, and they felt deeply appreciated. It was a moment they would cherish forever, knowing that their adventures had made a real difference.

As the festivities continued, Danny noticed Marcel standing at a distance. Marcel was watching the celebration with a wistful expression on his face, looking like he wanted to be a part of the joy but felt out of place.

Danny decided to approach him.Walking over with a warm smile, Danny greeted Marcel. He wanted to show that there were no hard feelings and that everyone, including Marcel, could share in the happiness of the day.

"Thank you for doing the right thing ,"Danny said to Marcel. "The path to truth might not always be easy, but it's never too late to change and find a new way."

Marcel nodded gratefully."You showed me that seeking the truth can come from the heart, not just from a necklace or power, " he said. "I'll use my skills to uncover the mysteries of the world in a different way."

With those words, Marcel began his own journey toward redemption. He realized that finding the truth was not about owning something valuable, but about understanding and compassion. This new perspective gave him a sense of peace he had never felt before.

Marcel knew that his past actions didn't define his future. Embracing this new outlook, he decided to make amends and help others, proving that he had changed. It was the start of a new chapter in his life, one filled with purpose and kindness.

The celebration lasted late into the night , with music, laughter, and friendship filling the air. Everyone was in high spirits, enjoying the joyous occasion. Danny and Katy joined in the festivities, dancing under the starry sky, feeling a deep sense of happiness.

As they danced, Danny and Katy's hearts were filled with gratitude for the people of Midrock and for the adventures that had brought them to this moment. They knew that this was just one of many wonderful memories they would create together in their journey as young detectives.

As the night came to an end , Danny looked out over the town he cherished. The moonlight cast a gentle glow over Midrock , making it look even more beautiful. He felt a sense of peace and satisfaction, knowing that this place held so many special memories for him.

Danny knew there be many more mysteries to unravel in the future. However, he was confident that with Katy by his side and the unwavering support of the people of Midrock, there was no challenge they couldn't overcome together.

As the young detective and his loyal companion Katy made their way home, they felt a deep connection to the town of Midrock. They knew that their hearts were linked to a place where mysteries were solved, friendships were made, and dreams came true. The town had become a part of their lives in a meaningful way.

With hearts full of joy and gratitude , Detective Danny eagerly anticipated the future. He was excited about the next thrilling adventures that awaited them. He understood that the story of "The Mystery of the Missing Necklace" was only the start of an amazing journey filled with new mysteries to uncover.

Lessons learned from this story

1. ***The Power of Perseverance***: The story emphasizes the importance of persistence and determination in solving mysteries and overcoming challenges. Detective Danny and Katy never give up, even when faced with cryptic clues and obstacles along the way.

2. ***The Value of Friendship***: Danny and Katy's strong bond exemplifies the significance of friendship in facing adversity. Their teamwork and support for each other enable them to overcome the mystery together.

3. ***Discovering True Power Within***: Marcel's desire for the necklace's mystical powers teaches the lesson that true strength and wisdom come from looking within oneself, rather than seeking external possessions or abilities.

4. ***Compassion and Redemption***: The story showcases the power of compassion and understanding. Danny and Katy show empathy towards Marcel, leading him towards redemption and a change of heart.

5. ***The Importance of Community Support***: The town of Midrock's unwavering support for Danny and Katy illustrates the significance of a caring community. Their recognition as celebrated detectives reinforces the value of having people who believe in and uplift one's efforts.

6. ***Lessons in History and Knowledge***: The story highlights the value of historical knowledge in solving mysteries. Investigating the past provides crucial insights into the necklace's origins and its significance.

7. ***Embracing New Adventures***: The story leaves readers with a sense of excitement for the future.Danny and Katy's readiness for new adventures shows the joy and growth that come from continuing to explore and face new challenges.

Overall, the story of "Detective Danny And The Mystery of the Missing Necklace" imparts valuable lessons about determination, friendship, compassion, self-discovery, and the positive impact of community support, creating an inspiring and heartwarming narrative for readers especially kids.

www.ingramcontent.com/pod-product-compliance
Lightning Source LLC
Chambersburg PA
CBHW081934120726

47997CB00010B/3135